On the very day that Oaf turns eight he is sent out to make his own way in the world, his only possessions the three gifts his aunt has left to him. The first gift is simply one word: fifty-fifty. The second is a cap of scarlet leather, said to be magic. The last is the promise of a treasure. "There is no known road to this treasure and the way is steep," said his aunt, "but one day you may be led to it."

Joined in his travels by a crow, a dog, a cat, a rat, and a fox, Oaf finds that the way is steep indeed, and filled with hardship and peril. But guided by his wise aunt's gifts and supported by the friendship of his companions, Oaf finds the courage to confront a most wicked master.

With her own celebrated gifts of language and imagination, Julia Cunningham spins a timeless tale in which innocent goodness overcomes treachery and evil. Oaf will win readers' hearts and stand in memory as one of the most staunchly endearing young heroes in children's literature.

ALSO BY JULIA CUNNINGHAM

The Treasure Is the Rose
Burnish Me Bright
Candle Tales
Dorp Dead!
Far in the Day
Macaroon
Onion Journey
Viollet
The Vision of Francois the Fox
Maybe, A Mole
Come to the Edge
A Mouse Called Junction
Flight of the Sparrow
Wolf Roland

~ *by Julia Cunningham* ~

OAF

illustrated by Peter Sis

ALFRED A. KNOPF NEW YORK

288014

THIS IS A BORZOI BOOK PUBLISHED BY ALFRED A. KNOPF, INC.

Text copyright © 1986 by Julia Cunningham
Illustrations copyright © 1986 by Peter Sis

All rights reserved under International and Pan-American Copyright
Conventions. Published in the United States by Alfred A. Knopf, Inc.,
New York, and simultaneously in Canada by Random House of Canada
Limited, Toronto. Distributed by Random House, Inc., New York.
Designed by Eileen Rosenthal
Manufactured in the United States of America
2   4   6   8   0   9   7   5   3   1

Library of Congress Cataloging-in-Publication Data
Cunningham, Julia.   Oaf.   Summary: Eight-year-old Oaf, seeking his for-
tune with a band of talking animals, seeks to rescue five dwarfs and a dancing fox from their cruel master.
[1. Animals—Fiction.   2. Fantasy]   I. Sis, Peter, ill.
II. Title.   PZ7.C9167Oaf   1986   [Fic]   85-14654
ISBN 0-394-87430-7   ISBN 0-394-97430-1 (lib. bdg.)

For Constance Cunningham
sharer of magic
and long found a treasure
with Oaf's and my love

OAF

CHAPTER ONE

The boy loved his aunt. He not only loved her. He listened to her, and every word she said he believed.

His right name was Olaf but one day when he was five some village children passed by and found him talking to the neighbor's pig and one of them shrieked, "Look at that stupid oaf and his pig. One's as smart as the other."

Olaf, hurt for himself and his pig friend, ran into the house and encircled his aunt with both arms, pressing his face against her apron to hide the oncoming tears.

She had heard the jeers and, loosening his grip around her waist, she knelt to just his height and looked into his eyes. "Little one," she began, "an oaf is how you find one and I find you handsome as a prince, alert as a fox, and sweet as a sugar cake."

So ever afterward Oaf was her special name for him and he was proud to answer to it.

Now, on the very day he had grown to be eight she took him in her lap, his long legs dangling to the floor, and he felt a deep sadness in her embrace.

"Dear Oaf," she said, "I must leave you."

"You must leave me?" he whispered.

"Yes. I do not wish it so but I am very old and it is time. Before I go I will give you three gifts."

Oaf put out both hands, palms upward, in case they might prove heavy.

She smiled. "No, dear one. The first has no weight and its value is what you make of it."

He smiled back, the tenderness between them as always making him happy. He left her lap, dropped his hands to his sides, and stood at attention so that she would know he was ready.

She pulled him toward her and kissed him on the left cheek and then on the right and said one word, "Fifty-fifty."

"I see," said the boy, not really seeing at all.

She stroked his thatch of straw-colored hair. "The second gift is this cap." She took from her broad pocket a scarlet cap of leather, shaped to a peak, and fitted it to his head. "I made it for you long ago and you may have need of its magic."

The boy laughed. He was skilled at pretending. His aunt had taught him, reading him books, showing him how to form shadows of strange creatures on the white walls with his hands, helping him to learn the true meanings of sounds and signals, how the birds and animals speak to each other. And now she had given him a pretend cap, calling it magic because it was more pleasurable to imagine it was.

He hugged her and this time, he didn't quite know why, he wanted to hang on forever.

She gently pried his arms from around her neck. "The last one is a treasure. There is no known road to this treasure and the way is steep, but one day you may be led to it."

He didn't question her. He never had. He simply believed. "The way is steep," he repeated so that the words would stay with him.

She put on her best black hat, hung her rusty-brown purse over her arm, and opened the front door to disappear forever. She looked into his eyes once more and he knew that her gifts would guide him. She handed him a small packet of sandwiches and walked quickly through the doorway, her back turned to him, but he knew without seeing them that tears filled her eyes. Then she hurried off so fast he had only an instant to wave her away. She did not echo his gesture and now he stood alone, alone and wondering.

Suddenly, as he looked down the long road to the beginning of a world he could not even imagine, he wished he could squeeze it all small again to just the size of this house, this single tree, this square of flowered grass with his aunt at the center. For the last time he looked long at the round kitchen table, the two chairs across from each other, the three pans on the old black stove, the cupboards, now empty, the calendar where he had memorized his numbers, the small, bare bed under the one window where he had slept safe each night.

Then, as quickly as his aunt, he turned his back to all

of it and closed the door after himself, gently.

He pondered her words. Three gifts, the peculiar instruction "fifty-fifty," the cap—he touched it to be sure it was still there—and the promise of treasure.

He glanced around him. The open meadow and the nearby forest were all he saw and he had known them forever. Nothing different, no surprises. Well, he had best be off to find some.

He decided on the forest and strolled through the first stand of oak trees. Same trees, same squirrels, but suddenly a new sound burst through the pine branches just overhead.

"Caw! Caw! Go home to your maw!" shrieked the large black bird who flapped his wings so close they tickled Oaf's ears.

Oaf rubbed off the tickle. "I haven't got either," he said.

"Either what?" croaked the crow.

"A maw, whatever that is, or a home. I just left mine."

"How foolish of you. What for?"

Oaf wished so hard he hurt, wished to be back with his aunt just fitting a round of cheese to a square of bread for his lunch and then she would put out blue bowls for each of them and fill them with blueberries. Or strawberries. Or huckleberries. Any kind would do just so he could be there with her in her warm kitchen again.

"She had to go away," he murmured to the crow, turning sideways so the bird wouldn't see the two tears that dropped from his eyes.

But the crow was quick and missed nothing. "No need to

snivel," he said harshly. "Here—let's play catch." He swooped across Oaf, snatching his cap, and perched on the nearest branch, just out of reach.

"Throw it here!" Oaf shouted, his tears evaporating on his cheeks. "That's one of the gifts she gave me."

"And the others?" the crow jeered. "A pocketful of gold perhaps or a diamond as big as a walnut?"

Oaf stamped his feet in the dust. "Of course not!"

"What then?"

"One word and a treasure."

"You can keep the word. I've more than enough of those, but the treasure?" He cocked his head to one side. "I'll trade you your cap for that."

"But I don't know what it is. She didn't tell me."

"In that case I'll just stow this cap where it will make a cozy nest for some cronies of mine next spring." With that he settled it onto a very thin branch and flew to the ground.

"How about that?" the crow said smugly.

For reply Oaf began to climb the tree. He had reached the second fork and was just stretching out his right arm toward the cap when his feet slipped and he tumbled down through the leaves and twigs, landing flat on his back.

When the boy's eyes stayed shut the crow fluttered his wings like fans across the still face.

Then swiftly he flew up into the tree, retrieved the cap, and returned. He fitted it as securely as he could to the boy's head and stationed himself on the boy's stomach, watching for the slightest sign of revival.

He fitted it as securely as he could to the boy's head and stationed himself on the boy's stomach.

He hadn't long to wait. Oaf sat up slowly, dislodging the crow. Returning to himself, he patted his head, pleased to discover the cap, and then started to untie the packet his aunt had sent with him.

"I'm sorry," said the crow, swaying from one foot to the other.

Oaf seemed not to have heard him as he drew out a very thick sandwich of cheese and pickle. He had almost taken the first bite when he remembered his gift, that one word, *fifty-fifty*. He looked at the sandwich. Was this what his aunt had meant? Maybe. He carefully divided the square of bread into two equal portions and handed one to the crow.

"But I did you a bad turn," protested the astonished bird.

Oaf smiled, his mouth full of cheese and pickle, and just managed to say, "Fifty-fifty."

CHAPTER TWO

$\mathbf{A}$s Oaf walked down the road which was lined with tall poplars, sometimes jumping across the shadows they cast in the golden dust as he passed, he noticed that the crow was still with him.

"Why are you following me?" he asked finally. "We ate the sandwich."

"I'm not exactly following you. I'm going with you."

"Why?"

The crow's answer was gruff. "Because of the treasure," he said.

"Well, come along," said Oaf. "But it is doubtful if I will ever find it. I'm only looking because my aunt wanted me to."

"You mean maybe there isn't one?" The crow was not used to foolishness of this kind.

"Who knows?" Oaf replied.

"All very vague," the crow muttered as he flew three trees ahead of the boy and then waited for him to catch up.

So they journeyed until the sky had almost turned evening and their horizon had become the edge of a village.

"I'm tired," said Oaf.

"And so you should be, being wingless," said the crow. "I walk as little as possible."

Oaf only half heard the crow's remarks as his eyes scanned the small houses on each side of the first street. Lines of light shone through the shutters and once he heard singing as though the people inside might be having a party. He thought back to his own lost bed and wished he were once again under the shelter of his blue down coverlet.

"How about here?" came the raspy voice of the crow. He was pointing to a small shed in the middle of a vegetable garden. "Ready-made supper, too." Oaf saw the tops of carrots and the line of tomato vines. He realized he was hungry.

Cautiously he opened the door of the shed. It was crowded with tools—shovels, rakes, hoses, and other things he had no names for. The crow peered over his shoulder.

"Just about enough room for an outsized rat," he commented.

Oaf laughed. "A bit better than that but not much," he agreed. "Let's get our supper."

"Fine," said the crow. "I'll keep watch while you gather."

It was almost dark now and Oaf made a few mistakes, detaching a large squash that was not ripe and getting stung by a row of nettles that hedged the tomato vines, but finally he and his friend sat down on the grass to eat. The crow complained in a lighthearted way but ate his share.

After chewing the last bite of carrot, the boy yawned, rubbing his eyes to keep them open. He crawled into the shed and curled himself between a crate and a bag of seed. Sleep had nearly captured him when the angry "Caw! Caw!" of the crow startled him completely awake.

He thrust his head through the half-open door of the shed. "What's up?" he called.

"A filthy mongrel, that's what's up!"

Oaf glimpsed a dim flurry of feathers and the leaping of a beast so white he might have been a ghost dog. The crow had just arrowed for the cringing animal's eyes when Oaf threw himself between them, gripping the dog around the neck with one arm and fending off the crow with the other.

"Stop that!" he shouted to the crow. "Can't you see the dog's afraid of you?"

"What I see," said the crow, landing on the ground at Oaf's feet, "is skin stretched over bones to make a joke."

Oaf felt something wet touch his right hand. The dog was licking it. "He's no joke," said the boy. "He's lonely."

The crow sighed. "I'm going back to sleep. Good night. Pick me some grapes for breakfast." With that he flew to the roof of the shed and tucked his head under his wing.

Never letting go of the dog, Oaf crawled back into the tool house. He squeezed himself again next to the bag of seed but this time the dog squeezed with him.

"There really isn't much room here," he heard the dog whisper. "I'll get out."

Oaf felt the shivers that ran down the animal's spine. "No, indeed. With me it's fifty-fifty." And with that his eyes closed in sleep.

"Stop that!" he shouted to the crow. "Can't you see the dog's afraid of you?"

CHAPTER THREE

The next morning Oaf poked the dog awake and called the crow from his perch on the shoulder of a scarecrow.

"Why so early?" asked the crow, who had been dreaming of emeralds.

"Because it's only fair."

"What do you mean?" said the dog, who was having trouble with fleas.

"Since we helped ourselves to those vegetables last night we should even it out somehow."

"How?" said the dog, scratching behind one ear.

"Before we leave we'll do a little weeding to pay for what we took."

The crow laughed raucously. "You really are an oaf, you know. Pay, repay. You'll never get anywhere with that way of thinking."

"Maybe not," said Oaf, "but my aunt said fifty-fifty. That's what she said and that's what I do. Besides, how did you know my name?"

The crow shrugged. "I didn't. That's just what you are."

"Look," said the dog, who was grateful for last night's company, "I'll dig weeds and the crow can gather them and fly them over to another field."

"Good strategy," said the crow, "except that leaves our fifty-fifty friend here with nothing to do but smell the flowers."

"Oh, he can do his share all by himself."

Oaf was very pleased by the compliment and went to work immediately.

In an hour they had cleared the entire patch.

"We'd best be off," warned the crow. "I can hear the water running in the farmer's kitchen."

"And I can smell the coffee," said the dog.

"Yes," Oaf agreed, "let's go."

They headed down the road toward the center of the village. Just ahead Oaf saw a jumble of people and little stalls piled high with apples and cabbages, beets and onions, potatoes and celery, and others with flowers and necklaces, pots and kettles, towels and trousers. He had never seen so much before. He just stood in the middle of it all and stared.

But not for long.

Suddenly something hit him on the side of his jaw, then a blow to the back of his knees. He fell forward. Looking up, his chin in the dust, he saw a circle of feet, some shod, others bare and brown with dirt. He lifted his head. A round wall of boys surrounded him.

"What you doing here?" sneered one.

"Where'd you get that funny hat?"

"Empty your pockets and be quick!"

Someone hauled him upright and thrust his hands in Oaf's pants pockets.

"How about this? He uses acorns for money!"

"And pebbles!" shouted another.

Oaf stood there, his inside-out pockets dangling, his cap crooked. He heard the dog growling and the crow cawing but how could they defy such a group of tormenters? He knew, too, that the boys would soon tire of making remarks. The next thing would be a beating and he the victim.

What could he do? Then he thought of his aunt and what she had told him. Fifty-fifty. He would give as good as he had been given.

His fists flashed out and landed in the eye of one of the bullies and on the chin of another. The two stepped back, breaking the circle. Oaf's feet struck at the nearest legs. Howls of pain cut the surprised silence. Blow after blow whirred around him and he didn't even feel the punches that lighted on his body. The circle had widened now and some of the boys were retreating up the street.

"Come on," said the leader, who had a black eye. "This isn't any fun." He aimed a farewell kick at Oaf but was met with a butt in the stomach.

Finally free of his assailants, Oaf rubbed his bruises and tried to slap the dust from his clothes.

"Sorry I couldn't be of any help," said the crow. "I'm too small." He glanced at the dog, who was standing with his

His fists flashed out and landed in the eye of one of the bullies and on the chin of another.

head down. "Not like some others," he added.

The dog trotted toward the nearest corner and would have turned it if Oaf hadn't called out to him, "Don't go!"

The dog raised his head and looked at the boy, straight into his eyes. Then he spoke. "You don't want me around. I'm a coward. Always have been ever since they threw me out of the house because they said I ate too much."

"And did you?" asked the crow, still indignant at the dog's refusal to defend Oaf.

"Never got the chance."

Oaf had never been really hungry, although he was beginning to experience a definite vacancy in his insides. But as he looked at the dog's ribs, each one showing sharp under his skin, and his bony neck, he realized that this animal had always been hungry.

"Let's figure out what we are going to have for supper," he said, and stroked the dog's back with both hands.

"That's easy," said the crow. "You two meet me later at the far edge of the village. I won't be long."

The crow's promise was well kept. In twenty minutes he called a proud caw to his two companions as he slid to the ground and released from his beak a kerchief bulging with provisions. Half a loaf of bread, a chunk of yellow cheese, two plums, and a banana. Oaf carefully divided the meal into three parts and although the dog confessed he was not too fond of fruit he ate his allotment with eagerness.

"How did you do it all?" asked the dog admiringly.

"Simple," answered the crow. "I love to steal. You

should have seen my hoard when I was nesting close to a palace. Even had a sapphire ring and a moonstone necklace."

He was so immersed in these remembered images he failed to notice the shock in the dog's eyes or the surprise in Oaf's.

"I'd have been given a beating for that," the dog said.

"That's because you've never been free—until now," commented the crow. "You couldn't choose. As for me, I'm attracted to things that glisten. I collect them."

"You mean you can't help it?" asked Oaf, who had never even imagined taking what wasn't his.

"Something like that." The crow was becoming a little uncomfortable. "But you ate well, didn't you? Without me you'd have gone to sleep empty as barrels."

The crow was tired of this discussion. "Before you bring me to trial let's just be grateful. What I do with my sapphires and moonstones is my business. But hunger's no joke. It's eat or die in my world. Tonight, thanks to me, we ate."

"But what happened to the jewels?" asked the dog, still not satisfied.

"A raccoon toppled the nest while I was away and I lost it all to a passing vagabond."

"Did you mind a lot?" said the dog.

"Not really," responded the crow. "What I took was taken. Fair enough."

Oaf was too puzzled to speak. Somehow the crow's

thinking just didn't fit what his aunt had taught him. He wished, as he had so often, that she were there so that he could ask her why.

But before this thought lengthened, a first thin rush of raindrops descended on them. "We'd better find someplace to spend the night and pretty soon," he said. He fastened the one button of his jacket and thrust his hands into his pockets.

"Saw a barn a little way off," said the crow, happy that the subject of his thieving had been diverted.

"Then lead on." Oaf was shivering now.

The sky had darkened with storm clouds.

The dog sniffed the rising wind. "Smells like a bad one."

"You mean storms have different smells?" asked the crow.

"Certainly," said the dog, pleased to show that at least he knew something. "This one is like scorched cloth, kind of cindery. Others—"

But suddenly they were pelted with a rush and a wetness that soon soaked through Oaf's clothes down to his under-wear and bedraggled the dog's fur into little strings. Only the crow seemed sleek and lively as ever.

They dashed as fast as they could, the crow leading, and at last they piled through the open door of the barn just in time to see a sizzle of lightning strike the nearest tree.

The dog cowered against Oaf.

Oaf sat down on a pile of hay and put his arm around the animal.

A terrifying yowl set his ears to ringing. He looked into the dimness but could see nothing except the outlines of the beams and the faint glow of the hay in the loft.

Then he heard the crow shriek, "Let go of my tail or I'll slice you up the belly!"

A second yowling and out of the obscurity leaped a black shape, its four legs spread, its ears laid back flat, and its red mouth open, all teeth showing. The creature landed on Oaf's chest, knocking him onto his back.

Little prongs like needles penetrated Oaf's jacket and stung him to action. He seized the attacker with both hands and tried to pull it off but the claws held. He got to his feet and, leaning over, attempted to shake it off.

By now the dog was barking and the crow diving so close Oaf could smell his feathers.

"Let me go!" Oaf yelled. "You're sticking me full of holes!"

"I can't!" came a muffled voice. "I'm hooked into you." But the intruder had quieted and no longer wriggled against the boy.

Oaf realized now that the black fur, the long whiskers, white in the dusk, the pointed ears, and the long black tail all together made a cat.

"Maybe I can help," said Oaf, anxious to be free of the cat's claws. One by one he pried them loose until the cat's four feet were clear of his jacket.

The cat started to jump away but suddenly the dog blocked her.

"You're not going anywhere!" the dog shouted, snarling.

The crow lighted on the dog's back and pecked him lightly. "What's the matter with you? Turning into a bully?"

The dog looked startled. "But dogs don't get along with cats. Didn't you know that?"

"I only know," said Oaf, "that I'm so tired I could sleep on nails."

The cat had retreated a few feet behind Oaf and was hissing, her back arched.

"Between the two of them," said the crow, "there's no sleep tonight."

Oaf sat down hard.

"What's the matter?" exclaimed the crow.

The dog's snarl changed to a worried sigh.

Even the cat was concerned and she rubbed her head on the back of Oaf's neck.

"Lie down," said the crow. "You're exhausted."

Oaf obeyed, not able to do otherwise, and he shuddered as little slivers of cold rose from the cracks in the floor.

"This won't do," said the crow, and he motioned to the dog.

The dog stretched himself beside the boy and signaled to the cat. The cat took the other side and the crow spread his wings and flew to the loft. Sixty trips he took, back and forth, carrying hay, until the three of them were covered with a golden blanket, and when he was finished he perched on top of the mound and closed his eyes.

. . . and when he was finished he perched on top of the mound and closed his eyes.

CHAPTER FOUR

The next day, almost before sunup, Oaf eased the stiffness from his arms and legs. Then he tried to smooth out the wrinkles in his clothes with the palms of his hands.

"You need a tailor," said the crow, ruffling his feathers.

The dog yawned widely and watched the cat stretch herself completely awake. "Feeling better?" he asked Oaf.

"Much. But if we are going to eat tonight I must find work. No more stealing."

The crow ignored this comment and regarded the sky. "Good day for flying," he said to no one.

"Then you'll be gone all day?" questioned the dog.

"Probably, especially if I am lucky enough to find a job. Shall we meet right here at sunset?"

The others nodded and the dog added, "We'll miss you."

A few minutes later Oaf's first call was at the town baker's back door.

The baker was just ladling the new loaves from the oven and placing them on a long wooden table to cool. Oaf's knock startled him into dropping one on the floor.

"Be blast!" he exclaimed. "Now I'll have to find a pauper to give it to."

"That might be me," said Oaf.

"And who in the devil's name are you?" The stout man's florid face showed a frown all over it.

"No one special," said Oaf. "But I do need a job."

"And what skills can you offer me?" The baker was tired and had thought of hiring an assistant but this waiflike boy didn't exactly fit the image he had in mind.

"I can offer you half of my strength, half of my common sense, and half of my willingness to work." Oaf hoped he had understood his aunt well enough so that these qualifications would impress the baker.

"And how about the other halves?"

"I keep those for myself. Otherwise I wouldn't be a person at all and of no use to you."

The baker scratched his beard, streaking it with flour. "Tell you what," he said, smiling, "I'll take you on but not for pay. You'll get your meals here with me, a cot to sleep on in the basement—it's always warm there, thanks to the ovens above—and Saturdays free. Mornings you'll have to go to school. We have a rule here in our village. Every child must go to school at least three hours a day."

"School?" said Oaf. "I've never been to school. My aunt used to hear my reading and even if I can't write much more than a few words at a time I can count from one to forever."

"That's all very well, but I'm in for trouble if you don't.

Either go to school—you can work extra hours when you return to the bakery—or leave the village. Take your choice."

Oaf considered the situation. The thought of the added hours was unpleasant but the image of school was more painful. What would it be like? He felt as though he were stepping into a dark hole.

"Well?" said the baker, who was longing to go to the café and smoke his pipe over a beer while the boy watched the ovens.

It was the thought of his companions that decided Oaf. He had only just arranged for them to have a home. He couldn't now take it away from them. "I'll take the job," said Oaf.

"Start now?" asked the baker, pleased with the bargain. At Oaf's nod he continued. "First you must sweep this room so clean a mouse would starve, then wash the pans, and after that you can bring up the sacks from the cellar."

Oaf suppressed a sigh. "Could I eat part of that loaf on the floor first?"

The baker consented, knowing that even a cheap favor put the other person under an obligation, and handed it to him. Oaf carefully broke off a piece from the end and put the rest aside to take back to his friends.

That was a very long day and the afternoon was nearly at an end when he staggered under the last sack, depositing it neatly with the others in the baker's bin. He was so weary he had to swallow hard to get down a portion of the potato soup the baker put out for him at suppertime. He asked if he might borrow a large bowl and was relieved when the man didn't question its purpose.

As soon as the baker was snoring Oaf joined the soup to what he had saved from the midday meal of stew and, with the half loaf under his arm, he hurried to the barn.

He was greeted with cheers from the dog and cat, and the crow tried to croak out a song until their laughter stopped him. They fell to the provisions so fast the bowl was soon empty.

"What now?" asked the crow after Oaf had told them of his new work.

"Come with me. I've been given the run of the basement, have my own room," he added proudly, "and there's lots of space for all of us."

As they quietly filled the room they saw the disappointment in Oaf's eyes as he looked at the cobwebs, the three-layered carpet of ancient dust on the floor, and the grime on the one tiny window so thick the moonlight from the outside was no more than a smear.

"We'll do something about this for Oaf," the cat whispered to the dog.

"Yes. Tomorrow."

"What's that about tomorrow?" Oaf asked sleepily, lying down on the cot.

"Good news," said the crow enigmatically as he watched from his perch on a pipe the boy drown into dreams.

The sun seemed to rise too soon to Oaf when he opened his eyes a few hours later. His muscles ached all over as though he had been kneaded along with the baker's bread but he got up quickly, patted the dog, stroked the cat, and smiled at the crow. He took the cellar stairs two at a time into the kitchen.

When they could hear his footsteps on the floor above they set to work. The dog had found a hose, attached to an outside spigot, that he pushed through the window and then managed to turn on with his teeth. The cat, who hated to get her paws wet, bravely waded into the shallow water and, a thick rag in her jaws, swabbed the gradually retreating stains on the cement flooring. The crow in the meantime had been busy whisking away the cobwebs, picking up the dust balls, and generally ridding the room of the smaller debris.

Oaf set about his chores, his mind filled with dread. Soon school would be a reality.

He had just finished cleaning the kitchen, the baker still out, when the crow appeared around the corner of the stairs. "Hist!" he said softly. "Come down for a minute and see what you see."

Oaf took up the bread he had saved from his breakfast and followed the crow into the basement. He was handing it to the dog to divide when the new brightness of the room struck him. "What have you done?" he exclaimed. "It's beautiful!"

"And look," said the cat. "You can even see the flowers blooming outside the window."

"And the stars at night," said the dog, who surprised himself with this unusually poetic notion.

Oaf grinned and was very happy that he had decided to

attend school, no matter how much he hated the ordeal. They had done this for him, and now he would do something for them. How true were his aunt's words. Fifty-fifty, the best way.

"Thank you. Thank you," he said, and told them his news.

The crow nodded, as if he approved, but the dog shook his head until his ears flapped. "Too bad," he rumbled. "Had a taste of that myself with my last master. He taught me obedience the hard way."

"Were you running away when you found us?" asked the crow, who was ever curious.

"Not exactly. He put me out."

"Why?" The crow again.

"You needn't answer that," cautioned the cat.

"He said I killed chickens." The dog lowered his head. "I didn't, of course. It was a fox."

The crow laughed. "So that's what you meant by eating too much."

Oaf broke the slightly awkward silence. "Well, if I'm going to become a scholar, I'd better find the school. See you tonight." With that he hurried upstairs.

The way was easy, for other children were coming out of their houses all along the street heading for the small brick building that was topped by a bell tower. The clanging of the bell made Oaf's ears hum. He hung back, watching.

Scuffling and pushing, the children formed two wavery lines, like an unrehearsed parade. A small boy fell to the ground and Oaf was certain he had been tripped by the boy in front of him. Two girls near the end of the line were pummeling each other while their friends urged them to fight. The voices, strident and shrill, seemed to cut into Oaf's ears and just as he covered them with his hands a short, rotund figure appeared on the threshold of the school's wide black door.

There was instant silence.

The man was dressed in a suit of muddied green and his round, tight face seemed stained by a paler wash of the same color.

"I don't allow this kind of behavior," he said, his voice almost a hiss. "The leaders will be punished."

Oaf wondered how he could tell who the leaders were since he had just arrived. He saw now that the man was tapping his right leg with a slim, pliant switch. He raised it and pointed slowly to three girls and four boys. Oaf realized he had chosen them at random.

"You will wait for me in my study," he said, "and the rest of you, dear children, may go to your classes."

Only the hurried tread of the group as they mounted the wooden steps, their gestures stilled and frozen, sounded in the clear morning air.

Oaf sat down hard on the curb. His feet suddenly seemed so heavy he wasn't sure he could lift them. "I can't. I just can't," he said, not aware that he had spoken aloud.

"Can't what?" asked a high little voice that seemed to come from beneath the floor boards of the house behind him.

The burble of a chuckle came from the same spot. Turning, Oaf saw a pointed head, two ears, then a long body and a longer tail emerge to sit facing him. A rat.

"Go to school," Oaf responded.

"Not easy, I'm certain of that." The rat studied the boy. "I've acquired my learning elsewhere."

Instantly the rat's words opened Oaf's mind to the memory of the evenings when he and his aunt used to sit in the same roomy chair to read together, and her warmth reached him so truly he was momentarily lost in the remembering of it.

"I can read, you know," he said finally. "My aunt taught me."

"I believe you," said the rat. "And more than that, I like you." Before Oaf could react the rat slipped into his jacket pocket. "Onward and upward!" came the muffled whisper. "Life's ladder is for climbing." The rat snickered at his own humor.

A few yards away Oaf sat down on the stoop of a shuttered house. What had he done? Now the baker would have to let him go and his comrades would have no more of the stews and soups that he had provided for them. And, worst of all, just when they had fixed a cozy, clean home for him, they would be forced to abandon it.

"She said everything should be fifty-fifty," Oaf murmured, so worried his teeth ached.

"Who said?" inquired the rat.

"My aunt. Don't you agree?"

"Not likely," responded the rat promptly. "In this life it's dog eat dog, cat eat cat, rat eat rat, or all three, if you wish.

Turning, Oaf saw a pointed head, two ears, then a long body and a longer tail emerge to sit facing him.

Dividing things only means that you lose the half you give away. But agree or not, let me help you. I am extremely bright and can provide you with ideas and solutions and entertainments as fast as I can flick my tail. You need me. I will be your school and teacher all in one."

Oaf had to smile.

"That's better," said the rat. "A smile improves your looks. As it does anyone's," he hastened to add, not desiring to hurt the boy's feelings.

"Need you or not," said Oaf, "you are welcome to come with us."

"Who is us and where are you going?" asked the rat, who preferred to keep his information filed and correct.

"Well," said Oaf slowly, "according to my aunt there is a treasure somewhere in my future."

"That aunt again," muttered the rat. Then he brightened. "Treasure? Where?"

"I don't know," said Oaf, rising. His friends must be told about school so that they could ready themselves for the new journey. He wished he could escape their disappointment in him.

When he entered the basement room the shining order of it was a reproach and Oaf told the incident of the school haltingly, his phrases uncertain. "I am sorry," he concluded. "Really sorry. I've ruined everything, lost our home, my job, and any hope of getting another."

The rat nibbled his ear.

"Oh, I almost forgot. This is the rat. He's joining us."

The three of them kept their distance from the rat, who now stood alone on the floor.

"Don't worry," said the dog. "I was beginning to feel trapped down here."

"There are too many of my kind in this town," said the cat, who had been forced to keep to the cellar by the native cats.

"And I haven't had any fun since we arrived," said the crow. "Not enough activity."

"Then I'll just say good-bye to the baker and we'll be off," said Oaf, greatly cheered. "Meet me at the gate of the village," and he vanished up the stairs before the rat could ask to go with him.

The cat and the dog and crow started out the doorway so fast they were in the back alley before the dog realized that the rat had been left behind. He paused and watched the rat race toward them. He waited for the rat to catch up.

"Oaf says that fifty-fifty is the best way to get along," said the dog. "So you can ride on my back as we travel. You can pay me back some other time—your half, I mean."

"I understand," said the rat, "and I will be sure to do just that," and he climbed up the dog's tail and seated himself between his shaggy ears. "Maybe," he said to himself, "maybe that aunt had something."

CHAPTER FIVE

The noon sun centered the sky as they came to the outskirts of a town twice the size of the one they had just left.

"Let's split up and scout for food," said the dog.

"Yes," said the cat, who had caught a sniff of fish from a nearby cottage, doubling her hunger. "We can meet behind this hedge."

"In an hour?" asked the rat, settling himself in Oaf's pocket.

"In an hour," agreed Oaf. He patted the rat's back with a forefinger.

Separating, they took off in different directions. Oaf and the rat headed for the town square, the rat wishing to investigate the cloud of noise that needled his curiosity.

A sudden quiet greeted them as they entered the wide cobblestone space that was bordered by Saturday market stalls and, behind them, two-story houses of some elegance. People were gathered in front of a raised stage where five puppets were cavorting in time to a drum. The drum major was a man so tall his head scraped the top of the stage. He

People were gathered in front of a raised stage where five puppets were cavorting in time to a drum.

was clothed all in black and his wide-brimmed hat concealed his eyes. Almost. But Oaf had glimpsed a glint of fire in their centers. The man's mouth twitched continually as though he were sending secret messages to the puppets, and Oaf thought he heard a kind of tiny whistling coming from between his long teeth. Without knowing why, Oaf shivered and looked away to free himself of the sight and sound of this strange person.

Now one of the puppets was singing in a reedy voice. Another was playing on a penny whistle. Oaf watched the man's mouth but it didn't move with the song. Someone else must be behind the squat line of puppets making them act and speak.

At the finish of the song the man left the stage and began to pass his black hat through the crowd. Many threw coins into it.

"Must have been a good show," said the rat. "Sorry we missed it."

"I'm not," said Oaf. "There's something wrong about it all."

"Wrong? Be more definite," said the rat.

"I can't. I just know."

The man, after drawing the curtains across the stage, had disappeared into the town inn.

"Want to find out?" asked the rat.

"How?"

"Their caravan is parked behind the stage. See? There's the head of their mule sticking out. Come on." The rat jumped from Oaf's pocket and dived under the platform so that Oaf could only follow. He had no sooner rounded the stage than the rat met him. "Come," he whispered. "There's a perfectly fine hole just under the window frame. Lift me up and I'll wriggle through."

"But you'll be alone in there. Without me, I mean."

"Maybe not. If there's a key in the door I can turn it. Then all you have to do is let yourself in."

The little animal pushed through the hole and shortly Oaf could hear a tiny scratching coming from the other side of the door. He was about to turn the knob when the mule dispiritedly shifted his weight in the shafts of the caravan.

"What's the matter?" Oaf asked.

The mule did not respond.

"Can't you speak?" Oaf asked.

The beast neither shook his head nor opened his jaws.

"The poor animal must be mute and deaf both," murmured Oaf. He hastily opened the door.

The rat beckoned to him to hurry and as Oaf stepped up and into the caravan he couldn't believe what he saw. "But they aren't puppets at all!" he cried out. "They're real!"

All five lay in a row across a wide bed, their stubby legs and short arms sprawled like a tumble of sticks.

"Dwarfs," said the rat. "Shall I wake them up?" And before Oaf could reply the rat began to squeak in the nearest one's ear. The dwarf did not stir so much as a toe. The rat tried again, this time louder. No reaction. He poked the dwarf lightly.

The dwarf's eyes half opened. "Ask the queen," he said in

tones so slurred only the quick senses of the rat caught it.

"What queen?"

The dwarf waved a wobbly arm in the direction of the end of the line and then fell back.

"Something very wrong here," said the rat. "Not normal, any of it."

Oaf looked over the five bodies and then noticed that the end dwarf had a thin straw crown on her head. "She must be the queen," he said, and very gently shook her by one shoulder.

Her right eyelid fluttered upward, then the left. "What do you want?" she said, her speech blunted.

"What's the matter?" asked Oaf. "Are you sick?"

"No, drugged. He always drugs us," was the reply. She turned her head to one side and covered her face with her hands as if to cancel the interruption.

"Why?" The rat's voice was piercing on purpose.

The little queen put one finger to her lips. "He'd break us in two for telling."

"You can trust me," said Oaf firmly.

The queen's face was pocked with grime and her eyes were dulled as much by hopelessness as drugs. "Can I?" Her doubts were obvious.

"Yes," said Oaf.

She smiled a wavery smile. "Perhaps I can. You have the look of innocence."

Oaf wondered what that was and with his thumb straightened the tilt of her straw crown.

"Why do you allow him to keep you under?" asked the rat.

She glanced at the sleep-distorted forms of her fellow dwarfs. "We're better off that way. He works us hard and feeds us scraps and if we complain, he is generous with his whip."

"Why don't you run away?" insisted the rat. "Misery is a poor choice."

"We tried once but our legs are short and he caught us before we had gone a half a mile."

"Are they your brothers?" Oaf asked to distract her from such a dark memory.

"Yes. We come from a noble family but the plague took our relatives, one by one." She paused to recover her breath. "Only we five were left. The master seized the prison tower for his evil practices and kidnapped us." Her speech blurred. "He took the royal apartment for his own personal use." The queen's face had blanched with exhaustion as she talked.

Oaf was about to speak again but the rat motioned to him to be quiet. "Quick!" he hissed. "Someone's coming!"

Oaf scooped up the rat and let himself out. He had no sooner taken five steps when he bumped into the master.

The man grasped Oaf by his shoulders and dangled him a foot off the ground, then released him with a push that nearly made him fall.

"I'm sorry," Oaf murmured, stepping out of the master's reach.

"What are you hanging around here for anyway? Answer

me!" As he wiped the spittle from his chin Oaf could smell the sourness of wine on his breath.

"Just passing by." Oaf's voice was faint.

The master grunted. "Good thing I'm full of cheer or I'd cuff you." He glanced at what Oaf had in his right hand. "Where'd you get that varmint? Make a tidy pincushion," he chortled. "Alive, of course."

Oaf didn't need the rat's tiny nip on his hand to tell him to leave. With a last look at the looming threat of the master, he took off as fast as his legs would go and didn't stop until he had left the town and rejoined the cat and dog behind the hedge.

While Oaf and the rat were gone the other animals had collected a feast.

"Better than nothing," said the dog, trying to hide his pride as he placed half a haunch of cold ham on a wide leaf.

"Stole it, did you?" inquired the rat rather admiringly.

"Lucky," said the dog. "Some rich people were having a sit-down picnic. Before they sat I managed to snatch this from the table."

The cat added a large packet of sardines and Oaf opened it.

"Fish is not a feast," commented the rat, but he ate as eagerly as the others. The crow, attracted by their colors, had made off with a long string of sugar rounds.

The sardines gone, the ham reduced to its bone, and the sugar lumps munched, they were ready to talk. The cat began. "So what happened in town?"

Oaf and the rat, taking turns, told of finding the dwarfs

and what they had learned of the tyranny of the master.

"We must rescue them," said Oaf.

The cat sniffed. "For what reason, may I ask? One takes one's chances in life."

"That's rather harsh," said the rat, "but I agree. I've had it hard and I'm not willing to meet up with harder."

"I, too, say no," said the dog. "Too dangerous."

The others tactfully avoided any mention of the dog's former admission of cowardice.

"How about you?" Oaf asked the crow.

"I'm not much help in situations like these," said the crow, "except as a lookout or a spy, but I am against any involvement with those puppet people."

"But they aren't just puppets!" protested Oaf. "They're as real as each of us."

"Sorry," said the rat. "Looks like none of us agrees with you. The vote comes to not even one of your fifty-fifties."

Oaf said no more but that night as the others crouched together for warmth he curled up against a tree trunk a little apart and in his mind he said good night to his aunt with sadness.

CHAPTER SIX

Oaf awoke from dreams that had cloaked him in shadows and instead of his usual "good morning," he silently left the group.

"I'll go and look for him," said the dog a little later, discovering that Oaf's sadness had become his.

"Wait a minute," said the crow. "I have an idea."

"Another?" said the cat, finding that she was unexpectedly cross.

"Let's hear it," said the rat.

"We all reacted against Oaf's wish to rescue the dwarfs for personal reasons. But we could follow the caravan."

"In case we change our minds, you mean?" asked the dog.

"A compromise?" asked the crow. "Sort of not saying no and not ruling out yes?"

"At least it might cheer up our friend," said the rat.

"I'm for it," said the dog.

"And I."

"And I."

With that settled they all trotted off in the direction Oaf had taken. But it was another hour before they found him.

In that hour Oaf had wandered first to the right, then to the left, without caring where, not hearing the crackle of the dead leaves under his feet. He felt betrayed by his companions. It was true that they had lived in a more wretched world than he, that they had known want and the bleakness of the rejected. They hadn't had someone like his aunt, who was his welcome for all his comings in and goings out. So instead of resenting their refusal to help the dwarfs he should try to understand.

Suddenly he was so homesick for the past, for the solace and serenity that had surrounded him in that plain, sweet-scented hut where his aunt by the light of one candle had been enough to disperse any darkness, he dropped flat on the ground and sobbed into the leaves.

When this spasm of grief was over he tunneled himself deeper into the fragrance of the leaf mold until he was almost covered. A brown beetle walked over his neck but he did not stir. Then something wet snuffled at one ear and what felt like a tongue licked his cheek. He raised his head. Looking directly into his eyes were those of a fox who seemed to be faintly smiling.

Oaf sat up. The fox sat down. They waited.

Oaf saw that a stiff black cord encircled the fox's neck, so tight he wondered that the animal could breathe. The fox's flanks showed his skeleton beneath his fur and his tail was bedraggled and torn.

Oaf tentatively stretched out his hand and when the fox didn't move he placed it on his head and very lightly patted him between the ears.

The fox's smile widened.

"It's been a long time," said the fox.

Now it was Oaf's turn to smile. "Why are you tied to a tree out here in the forest?" he asked. "And on such a cruel leash?" He reached for the rope to release him.

"No!" said the fox vehemently. "My master would kill me if I got free again. I tried once. I ran away. But he found me weeks later. He is more powerful than a hound spawned by the devil. He can smell me out no matter where I go."

Oaf saw that fear was the captor of the fox as surely as his master. He was about to argue with him when the dog appeared, closely followed by the cat, who had consented to be the mount of the rat. The crow dived down from the treetops.

Oaf noticed the dog's lips rise in a snarl and spoke quickly. "I want you to meet our new comrade," he said, "the fox."

"It's obvious what he is," said the cat, shrugging off the rat.

"No need to be disagreeable," said the crow, who had perceived the traces of tears on Oaf's cheeks.

The fox attempted to bow a greeting but the leash pressed too painfully against his throat.

"I'm not," the cat defended herself. "Just sensitive to unfortunate odors."

"Why are you tied to a tree out here in the forest?" he asked. *"And on such a cruel leash?"*

"I can't help that," said the fox. "I've been tied up now for two days and unable to clean myself."

The rat's tail twitched with impatience. He looked toward Oaf. "What's wrong with untying the animal?"

"He won't let me," said Oaf.

The fox studied each one and the strength of his scrutiny held them silent. "I am a dancing fox," he began. "The only one of my kind in the world as I know it. He raised me with a whip and I graduated from his lessons. I am being punished because I gave some stolen eggs to the dwarf people without his permission and I must stay here until he comes for me." Abruptly he stopped speaking. His ears pricked up. "Go—now! I hear my master's caravan!"

The dog was the first to move. He scooped up the rat in his mouth and ran. The cat was not far behind and even the crow, who could use the shelter of the trees, winged above them. Oaf came last and more slowly. He hated to leave his new friend. He had just rounded a large tree when he recognized the tall column of the master stride like a giant toward the fox.

"Happy to see me?" Oaf heard the master say and then he, too, ran out of sight after the others.

Panting, the dog sniffed the air, then signaled for them to halt. "It's safe now," he said. "His scent is gone."

"And here comes Oaf," said the crow. He nodded to the rat. "You tell him."

"It's bad news for the fox but good news for you," said the rat, anxious to hearten Oaf.

"Yes," interrupted the cat. "We all decided something together."

"To follow the caravan," the crow croaked.

"You might have let me tell it," said the rat.

"I'm hungry," said the dog.

"Who isn't?" said the cat, remembering the sardines.

"Then we must take to the road again," said the crow, "if we are going to tag behind the caravan, and he is sure to head for the next town."

"I'll find another job," said Oaf. "You're doing me the favor of staying close to the dwarfs, so it's only fair that I do you one."

The rat nudged the crow. "There goes old fifty-fifty again," he said, but his eyes were filled with fondness.

All that afternoon after their arrival in the next town Oaf sought work, going from door to door, from the sausage factory to the cheese shop to the vegetable stand to the livery stables. Some refused him politely, others told him to be off and fast. None gave him so much as an errand to do. As the sun began to lower he glimpsed the caravan and, concealed behind a stone wall, he watched the fox come out from the wings of a set that was hinged together with boards painted in garish splotches of red and blue and green. He danced like a dervish, his tail curling around him, while the dwarfs pounded out the beat on small, yellow drums. The pace was so fast Oaf could see the fox's chest rise and fall as though he were gasping.

The cat and the dog, watching from a nearby street, were

He danced like a dervish, his tail curling around him, while the dwarfs pounded out the beat on small, yellow drums.

becoming restless. "I can do as well as that," said the cat, and she leaped like a frog over the dog's back. The dog whirled, showing his teeth, and they whizzed round and round in a mock chase. The rat joined them, riding the dog as though he were a pony, holding to his ears as the dog pranced.

When at last they stopped, out of breath, there was a small clatter of coins on the pavement and they noticed that passers-by had formed a circle around them, laughing and pointing. The crow hurriedly picked up the offerings in his beak, one by one, and flew to a stack of wood, shoving them under a wide board.

"Supper!" chortled the rat. "Supper for all! Where is Oaf? He will have to do the shopping."

"I'll get him," said the crow, and he flew off.

In a few minutes, just before the people dispersed, Oaf, with the crow on his shoulder, appeared. As he pocketed the coins he heard one of the onlookers say, "They must be a troupe of performers with the boy as their trainer."

And that evening, as they sat around a small bonfire behind a deserted building, having savored everyone's favorite, Oaf repeated what he had heard.

The rat had only said "So?" when out of the darkness emerged the fox. They gathered close around him. The cat rubbed against one leg. The dog's tail wagged a welcome. The rat danced a brief jig while the crow waved his wings like banners. But it was to Oaf that the fox bowed.

"We have some cold chicken left," said Oaf. "Please take it."

"And my dessert cheese, too," said the rat.

"We're glad to see you!" said the dog quite unnecessarily.

The fox crunched down the chicken with relish. He passed up the cheese with a grin of thanks to the rat. "I heard what you reported," he said to Oaf, "and it sounds like a splendid idea. You would all together make a most original troupe."

The cat, who recognized the intelligence of the fox to be equal to hers, wished she had said it first. "But just jiggling ourselves in circles certainly wouldn't earn us a kingdom."

"No," the fox agreed gravely. "You need a plan, a script, and I am not unskilled in such inventions. Let's work on it." And until the moon was high they discussed and considered and argued and agreed and set a morning hour for the first rehearsal.

CHAPTER SEVEN

The sun had lost its earliness when Oaf spoke for the rest. "We can't wait any longer for the fox. If we're to give our first show this afternoon we must get ready." He turned to the rat. "Since your part is very small and you know how to get into the caravan, would you be willing to find out what has happened to our new friend?"

The rat, who knew that because of his size he would never be given the role of hero, consented cheerfully. He hesitated only long enough to hear Oaf tell them that he would handle the narration from the side since he was the only one who would be expected to talk.

He hurried off to the caravan. The master was nowhere in sight, so he let himself in through the same hole in the window frame. Just as before, the dwarfs were sprawled in a state of slumber. But where was the fox? Then he saw him, half hidden under a dirty blanket. He crept close. "What's the matter?" he whispered.

The fox opened one eye with difficulty. "He beat me for being out so late. He's got a temper like a cyclone, can't stop, and now I'm too lame to get up."

"What can I do for you?" asked the rat, feeling the weight of the fox's distress.

"Only one thing," said the fox weakly. "Tell Oaf to go forward with his show."

The rat felt his eyes sting. "We will dedicate the performance to you," he murmured almost inaudibly.

"Do that," the fox said, and turned on his side in great weariness.

The rat left the way he had come with only a glance at the dormant forms of the five dwarfs. When he had rejoined the others and told them of the fox's misfortune they agreed immediately that this, their very first theatrical venture, would be offered in the fox's honor.

But that afternoon, as they set up the little square stage they had put together with planks from a woodpile, they were tingling with stage fright. Oaf wasn't sure his voice would sound at all and the dog wished he were back in the forest, hidden by a thorn thicket. Only the crow was confident as he put on his costume that consisted of a long oblong of rag that might have once been white but was now streaked and stained. He thrust his head in a central hole and awaited his entrance.

To attract an audience before the play began, the cat and the dog leaped in circles, hopping up and down on their hind legs and waving their paws at the people who stopped to watch.

Oaf sat down on a crate by the side of the stage, his cap

perched valiantly on his head, and cleared his throat.

"If you would hear how a coward become a king," he began, his tones strengthening as he recalled the fox's instructions, "listen to my telling."

Five people paused to hear, then four more.

"First, meet the cast," he continued. "The Flying Terror." The crow, draped in his mottled sheet that gave his shape the look of a phantom, swooped through the air just above the onlookers' heads. They ducked. Then he returned to his place behind the low stage.

"The Princess," said Oaf, and the cat came gracefully out and curtsied.

"The Coward."

The dog, his head low, his tail between his legs, showed himself.

"And the story?" asked someone in the group.

"Once upon a time," Oaf started, "there was a beautiful Princess who had been taken captive by the Flying Terror." The crow croaked ominously. "No one dared to attempt her rescue, because fear of the Terror had spread like a plague throughout the land. But one day a Prince, so cowardly he walked on trembling legs, saw her leaning from the tower where she was imprisoned. She was so very beautiful he forgot to shake."

The cat was now perched on a box so that the dog had to look up at her. He had trouble controlling the real shaking of his legs but finally managed for the sake of the others.

Oaf now sang the small song they had composed the

night before with the fox's help and the dog pretended it was he doing the singing.

"If I could come near
And touch your sweet hand,
I'd find you so dear
I'd fall where I stand."

The audience laughed but their attention was so complete that there was not one shuffle of feet on the cobblestones.

Oaf continued the story. "The Prince became so enamored of the Princess he forgot the Terror and suddenly a great shadow fell upon him." At this point the crow dived downward, dragging the rag over the dog's body.

The dog, so absorbed in his part that he even imagined the cat really was beautiful, barked with shock and then, as plotted, flattened himself.

Oaf continued his narrative. "One morning when the clouds hung heavy and black above the Princess's tower, she told the dog who could not leave her that she had procured a poisoned mushroom and was going to eat it and die. The Prince begged her to live."

The cat bowed her head and clasped her paws to her chest. "No, I cannot," Oaf spoke for the cat. "Since you came, my heart has grown too big to contain me in this tower.

"She put the mushroom to her lips," continued Oaf in a hushed tone, "and was just about to eat it when—"

". . . suddenly a great shadow fell upon him."

Now the crow wheeled into the air, spiraling down and down until the end of the rag almost touched the cat.

"If I can't have you, no one will!" Oaf shouted for the Terror.

At this instant the dog-Prince leaped at the Terror, biting down on the rag. It fell to the stage and the crow was revealed, his disguise nothing more than a smudge on the stage. At this the Princess jumped down from her box and greeted the Prince with open paws.

"So ends the story," said Oaf, "and the Coward-No-Longer, who married the Princess, became the next King of her country."

Applause followed his last words and, taking off his cap, he passed it through the now sizable crowd. It was returned to him sagging with coins.

When the people had gone they took down the stage and retreated behind a building to count their earnings. None of them had seen the master, his face ugly with rage, return to his caravan.

CHAPTER EIGHT

"The first thing must be to get the fox's share to him," said Oaf as they sat in the shadow of their retreat.

"But he's a prisoner," said the dog.

"And what good will it do him to be rich with the master standing over him?" said the crow. "Seems to me we'd be better off to keep his share and follow the caravan as we planned."

"Really," said the rat. "It's all very simple. We free him and then give him his earnings."

The crow laughed jeeringly. "Simple, is it? It's you who are simple. Think the master is made of cheese and you can nibble him down to size?"

Oaf was confused. What was happening to the comradeship of his new friends? What would his aunt have said if she had been there? But the vision of his aunt was no help. She seemed to be waiting, silently, for him to clear the muddle in his mind. He waited and listened.

"We have to get him out," stated the dog. "Maybe the cat has a good idea."

They all suddenly realized that the cat had left the circle. "Well," said the dog, disgruntled, "that's a cat for you." "Don't be too sure," said the rat, determined, after the crow's insult, to disagree no matter what.

"Since when did a rodent defend his archenemy?" asked the crow, who was tired after his exacting part in the play.

Oaf stood up. "Stop it, all of you! Just stop it! The cat's gone. The fox can hardly move and we're stumped." He didn't know where to go from there and wished he could pull his cap over his eyes and hide from them all.

"No," said a silken voice. "Perhaps not." It was the cat returned. "I've good news. The master is in the inn on the way to getting very drunk. He's already slopped over a table muttering about what he called 'old prosperities.' "

"What are they?" asked the dog.

"Who knows?" said the crow. "Let's stick to facts. This gives us a chance to get the fox out. Come on, hurry."

"I don't believe there's any need for hurry," said the cat. "The master will be sodden until morning the way he looked to me." But the cat would not have been so certain if she saw the master now sitting at the table waiting for his dinner, his thin lips upcurved, showing his pointed teeth. And no one heard the words he muttered to himself. "I'll get them and make them dance to my tune or else."

The dog reached the caravan first. The rat ran up his tail and onto his back, squeezed once more through the window hole, then scurried across the snoring forms of the dwarfs to unlatch the door. They entered one after the other, Oaf last. He dropped to his knees beside the prone fox.

"Oh, my poor friend!" exclaimed Oaf, regarding the matted fur of the fox and the stripes where the whip had separated the hairs. "You must come with us."

"Yes," said the crow. "Otherwise your life span will be as brief as a May fly's."

"No one can survive what he does to you," enjoined the cat. "What happened this time?"

The fox sat up. "That is what puzzles me. I can't remember any faults in the show or, for that matter, complaints about the profits."

"Maybe he's just crazy," suggested the dog. "I had a crazy master once."

"Oh, do be quiet," said the cat. "We've more urgent things to talk about than your past."

"Later," said the fox kindly. The dog wagged his tail.

"Come with us," repeated Oaf.

"I'd like to," responded the fox. "But"—he looked at the rotund sleepers lined up by one wall—"what about them?"

"What about them?" said the rat sharply. He had begun to worry. They were wasting their chances. How drunk *is* drunk? he thought to himself.

"I mean," the fox went on, "I can't leave them here. If I go they go."

They all recognized that he would not yield to any persuasion on their parts but the lumpish drugged forms of the dwarfs seemed obstacles that no one could remove.

But the lumpish drugged forms of the dwarfs seemed obstacles that no one could remove.

The crow had to try. "Thanks to you we're a success," he began, "and just imagine how much better we would be with you as our star attraction. You said yourself that a dancing fox was unique in the whole world."

"Well, maybe not in the whole world," said the fox, nonetheless grinning with pleasure. Then his eyes took on a distance, as though he were held in a kind of inner vision, and as he began to speak, the words came slowly. "With the dwarfs themselves again we could create a little circus." He paused as the idea strengthened. "A little circus with all of us taking turns at juggling, knife throwing, sword swallowing, acrobatics, clowning—"

"If we could only shake them awake!" Oaf broke in, and just as he leaned down to grasp the collar of the queen, the caravan shook and shuddered as it rattled into life. The wheels underneath them bumped over the potholes of the road.

At first the shock held each one silent. The cat went rigid. The dog flopped onto his stomach. The crow's beak opened and stayed open. The rat's whiskers became rigid. The fox ground his teeth together. Only Oaf moved. He went to one and then the other of the dwarfs, shaking them by the shoulders until, ending with the last, he saw their eyelids rise. Their gaze was bleary. "You've got to stir yourselves," he said.

The crow guffawed. "Asking for a miracle? As well instruct a tree stump to run a race!"

"Shut up!" said the cat. "You're not helping anything."

"And you?" said the dog. "You tell us the master is dead drunk and out for the night and here we are, caged like a bunch of rats."

The rat glared at the dog and was about to nip his paw when the fox spoke. "Give up," he said. "We're finished."

Oaf was now flexing the legs of the dwarfs, one after the other. The queen kicked him by mistake. "Sorry," she muttered, her voice still glued by drowsiness.

"What the devil is that boy about?" said the fox. "Wake them up and we've only more trouble with the master."

"What are you trying to do?" asked the dog.

"Making trouble for the rest of us," said the crow. "Leave well enough alone and we might at least get ourselves out of this trap."

By now the dwarfs were emerging very slowly from their stupor. The one dressed as a court jester sat up and the three costumed as knights to the queen were waving their arms like swimmers in air.

"I'm trying to get them on their feet," said Oaf, quite out of breath with all his pushing and pulling.

"It's going to take more than that," said the crow.

"Wait!" exclaimed Oaf. "I'm going to try something else." To the amazement of his friends he shut his eyes tightly and pulled the rim of his cap down until it covered his nose and ears. Holding it with both hands he silently called on his aunt's promised magic. "I've got it!" He snatched the cap from his head and held it out as though they could all see the wonder it contained. "It is magic just like she said. We'll have to give it time but it's our only hope."

"Think he's going off like the dwarfs?" whispered the dog to the rat.

The cat looked sorrowfully at the crow.

By this time the dwarfs were clumsily hoisting themselves into sitting positions. "What's up?" asked the queen.

"We hope you are," retorted the rat.

"No need to be rude," she said, straightening her crown. "He keeps us so far under that sometimes we can't even follow the dance steps during the show."

A little moan came from the jester. He started to speak.

"Be quiet," commanded the queen.

"I can't. I've had enough of that."

"Then say it," said another dwarf. "Say it for all of us."

"He drugs us. We don't really know how. It might be the food or sometimes the water. But at least it's one way we can endure the master and what he makes us do." The jester glanced guiltily at the queen.

"I understand," said the dog.

"Understand what?" asked the rat sharply.

"Why they've never really tried to find out what the potion is or where he puts it. They can't stand up to him. I never could stand up to so much as a shadow."

"So it's time you bit down hard on a shred of courage, you and the dwarfs," said the rat.

"Listen," said Oaf. "Listen to me. Since no one knows where he plants the potion you've got to pretend to eat and drink whatever he gives you."

They all nodded.

"Spit out the food the minute he turns away and just ignore the water," counseled the crow.

"Agreed. Now can we sleep it out?" asked a dwarf, yawning widely.

In three minutes the five of them had returned to their dreams, even the queen.

The fox shrugged. "As well put your trust in a row of cabbages," he commented.

Oaf glanced at each one of his comrades. The dog was lying flat, head on paws, tail still. The cat had curled up in a round, only her eyes and ears visible. The crow's head was just ducking in under his wing. And even the fox had lost his alertness, his sight glazed with faraway ruminations.

Only the rat responded to Oaf's sadness. He said softly so Oaf could just hear him, "Magic or not the cap is very becoming."

"Do you think we have a chance?" Oaf asked in an undertone.

"Not much," said the rat.

"What will happen to us?"

"Get dumped in a quicksand bog most likely."

No one spoke again. Except for the drugged dwarfs no one slept and it was not just the bumps and jerks and rattles of the caravan that barred them from rest.

CHAPTER NINE

The only thing Oaf heard the next morning in the dawn light was an odd scraping sound coming from the one window. The caravan had stopped. He got up, stretched the stiffness out of his legs, and saw that the rat was enlarging the hole under the window frame, now bigger than himself.

"What are you doing?" Oaf asked.

"Gnawing enough room for the crow to get out," said the rat. "He's agreed to do a little scouting. Report the lay of the land."

Oaf wasn't quite sure what a lay of the land was but he respected the rat's shrewdness in all things.

"So we know where we are," added the rat with kindness.

"Ready?" said the crow, hopping up onto the window sill.

"If you are," said the rat, and he stepped aside.

The crow first thrust his head through, then followed with his sleek body. Oaf and the rat watched him spread his wings and take to the air. He vanished into a low cloud.

By this time the whole company was awake, even the

dwarfs whose round faces had lost their lumpish look.

"Good morning," said one.

"I'm hungry," said another.

The queen, smoothing her wrinkled skirt with great dignity, said nothing but she seemed pleased at the responsiveness of her band.

At this moment the door to the caravan opened and the master loomed large over them all. He was carrying a wide tray piled high with bread, bowls of what smelled like gruel, and a water jar. He put it down on the floor.

The cat had leaped onto the window sill and was concealing the hole with her body.

"Eat hearty," he said with a sneer. "It's not much but will keep you until we get to my tower. Then—" He didn't finish his sentence and Oaf saw the fox quiver.

"What the dangjiggle are you animals doing in here with my dwarfs?" he shouted. He glared at the cat and the dog, ignoring the rat. Then he saw Oaf. "Oh, yes, I remember. You villains stole my audience with your slipshod performance." He paused. "But maybe"—his anger had now become thoughtfulness—"maybe I could use you. Yes." He stroked his chin. "Maybe I could."

Now he was handing out corn cakes, two to each dwarf. "You can distribute the water for yourselves. I'll just lock you all in for safekeeping." He laughed shrilly and left the caravan, locked the door, and pocketed the key.

The queen hesitated, staring at the cakes in her small hand. The four other dwarfs did the same. "These would

"What the dangjiggle are you animals doing in here with my dwarfs?"
he shouted.

keep us safe from danger," she murmured. "I'm sure the sleeping potion is in them."

"That may be true," said the fox, "but our lives are threaded with terror and torment."

"Let's go down fighting," said the rat.

"I've no wish to go down at all," said the fox. "Nor has the queen. But the decision must be shared among them. All or none."

The little queen smiled at the fox. "Let me hear from your companions before I act."

"I am cautious," said the cat.

"I say take a chance," said the dog.

"And you?" She directed her question to Oaf, who wished his aunt were there to answer this appeal. Then he saw her in his mind and heard her voice. "I will give you three gifts. The first has no weight and its value is what you make of it. Fifty-fifty."

"Fifty-fifty," he said aloud, so real was her invisible presence.

Now it was the fox who smiled. "If I may interpret my friend's remark," he said, "he means that we all may, if we are extraordinarily lucky, have a fifty-fifty chance."

Instantly the queen threw the corn cakes under the wide bed. The four other dwarfs did the same.

"But," advised the fox, "you must pretend to be drugged or the master will know what you have done."

The five nodded solemnly.

A gentle caw sounded at the window, followed by a very

ruffled crow. "It's awful out there," he said, almost breathless. "The wind never stops. Nothing to stop it. No trees, no bushes. Flat, flat, flat."

"And the people?" asked the dog.

"People! You could wish for the worst of them. Not a living soul. No villages. No farms. Never saw such a country. Nightmarish."

"Then what I feared is coming true," said the fox. "We're not too far from his tower where he lives when he isn't touring."

"My tower," corrected the queen but no one seemed to hear her.

"You mean he is taking us there?" questioned the cat, licking first one paw and then the other in her nervousness.

"Seems likely," said the rat.

Oaf, sensing the fox's distress, stroked his back. "There's more, isn't there? Something you haven't told us."

The fox placed a forepaw on Oaf's arm. "Yes. That tower is the devil's own domain. I know. The dwarfs know."

"You mean the master?" asked the dog.

"Who else?" said the crow.

"Tell them," said the queen.

The crow spread his wings and balanced from leg to leg. "Yes. No time for secrets."

"I had hoped to spare you," said the fox, "but I see that I can't. Once inside that tower he will have total power over us. There will be no escape. And if anyone tries he will be put in a hanging cage on the outside wall and either left to rot or be—he will never know the moment—plunged down to his death. I know. It happened to me."

"But you're still here," said the dog.

"Only because he needed me for his show. But I spent five days and nights suspended with no room to either lie down or sit up." He shuddered, his voice low and strained. "No food. No water. Only the wind that ripped through my fur like burning arrows and the sound of my own crying."

The rat went to the fox and leaned against him. The dog licked the tip of the fox's tail and the cat hid her eyes in her paws.

When he next appeared the master pushed his way in so abruptly the dwarfs scarcely had time to close their eyes, pretending drowsiness.

"Hungry are you, little ones?" he addressed them all. "Well, we'll be on short rations for a while. No need to fatten you up." He put down on the floor a tureen of beans and six plates. "The animals among you can lick the bowl, that is if there is any left after my performers have served themselves." He chucked the queen under her double chin. "How are you, bright eyes?"

She half-opened her lids and stared above his head.

"Get the joke?" he asked the fox.

The fox only swished his tail.

The master pulled out a strand of the queen's hair. She smothered a gasp of pain. "I've plans for you and your distinguished courtiers," he said. "My show has been limping for a long time, thanks to your lack of artistic energies and general ugliness, and now that I've seen what these others"—he glanced malevolently at Oaf and the animals—"have to offer, well, my pockets will fill again. But I won't let you go for nothing. Not me." With this he left the caravan, locking the door behind him.

Oaf went to the window and looked out. His faith in their having a fifty-fifty chance was melting as surely as snow on a griddle. He scanned the vacant landscape. His heart thudded double time. The horizon was no longer blank. Far off, but not far enough, rose the black pinnacle of a tower. Just behind it he could glimpse the parapets of the queen's castle, green with an overgrowth of vines, a few tumbled stones gaping like hollow eyes in the walls. Only the tower seemed real, the rest part of the queen's dreaming. He turned quickly away and said nothing to the others. The fox caught his unease but he, too, said nothing.

So the hours passed in silent depression. Even the rat seemed bound into stillness and the crow's head drooped, his beak almost touching the floor.

The first words came from the cat, her ears pricked upward. "He's coming. Watch out."

The dwarfs lay limp.

The man was grinning as he filled the entrance. He seemed to have swollen as though his evident glee had enlarged his body. He shoved the nearest dwarf with his foot. "Get up, you scum. All of you. Get up!" He cracked his whip.

The dwarfs, startled out of their simulated lethargy, jumped to their feet.

"That's right. You'll show a little life or be stung into it." The whip whistled over their heads. "Now, hurry out of here. We've come to a parting. Yes, you too, Queenie. The boy goes later when I've learned his tricks with the animals."

Two of the dwarfs began to whimper. One tried to crawl into a corner but was yanked by his arm to the doorway. "Not on your life," growled the master. "I promised to deliver all five of you—even though five don't even make one," he added cruelly.

Now they could see from the open door two people, a man and a woman, so wide they might have been made of huge blobs of dirty clay. Long, black hairs sprouted from their chins and their mouths were slack. They stood by a crude wagon attached to an ox as mud-streaked as they.

The master pushed the dwarfs from the caravan and as they tumbled every which way into the dust he followed. Oaf, the fox, the crow, the dog, the rat, and the cat crowded the opening to watch and listen.

"Here are your beasts," the master said. He lifted them up by their collars into a ragged line with a pinch for each. "They'll work for you if you give them a taste of this, generously." He flicked his whip so close to the queen she could feel the whirr of its passing.

Then the woman spoke, her speech thick. "Dwarfs they are, mighty puny to work our potato fields."

Now they could see from the open door two people, a man and a woman, so wide they might have been made of huge blobs of dirty clay.

The master continued as though she hadn't spoken. "I'd advise you to chain them together at night. They're like all animals, have to get used to you. Want to see them dance?"

Now three of the dwarfs were crying softly.

In the caravan the others had been shocked into helplessness.

"They're spoiled," said the master. "You'll want to keep their rations down."

"I know how to lean them," said the woman, smiling hideously.

The man grunted. "Clever wife, I have." He slapped her on the back and she wobbled with pleasure.

"Seems to me by the look of them," said the man, "you're asking too much. I've never yet been taken for a Simple Simon."

"No," hummed his wife complacently, "he's no Simple Simon. Best listen or lose the deal."

"Look!" whispered the rat to Oaf. "Look at the queen!"

What they saw was the queen suddenly waltzing clumsily, unlike her usual grace, swaying backward and forward, her plump arms high, her fingers snapping like castanets. She sang off-pitch as she stumbled about in three-quarter time.

> "I'm a little bumblebee
> Buzzing you and buzzing me,
> Join in my jollity."

She repeated the last line, the words now clear, now slurred. "Join in my jollity!"

At this her four companions began to imitate her gyrations, and as they spun they bumped into each other, giggling foolishly.

"They're loony!" shrilled the woman.

The queen fell to the ground. The four collapsed beside her.

The master threw his whip across them but their only reaction was another spurt of giggles.

The man spat angrily. "Curse you! You've tricked us. You promised slaves and you give us crazy pygmies. Take them and be damned to you!" He stomped back to the wagon, the woman with him, and soon they were lumbering into the desolate flatness and out of sight.

The master was just about to flog the prone dwarfs when Oaf spoke up. "You drugged them. They are guilty of nothing. And if you injure them now they will never be of any use to you."

The master paused. "I'll teach you, all of you, to resist me when we get to my tower. Just you wait!"

He pushed and kicked and shoved the five dwarfs back into the caravan and slammed the door.

When the dwarfs had been comforted with pats all around Oaf congratulated the queen for her cleverness. She tried not to show her gratification and in the next instant her smile was erased.

"Perhaps," said the fox gravely, "perhaps they would have been better off with those monsters than with death in the tower."

CHAPTER TEN

That very evening, as the sky darkened with the going down of the sun, filling what had been scarlet and orange with a murky purple, a long shadow striped the hill ahead of them.

The cat, watchful at the window, was the first to see it. "There's the tower," she said, her purr silenced.

The fox joined her. "Yes," he breathed, and said no more.

The dwarfs, nearly recovered from their fright, formed a small circle and, moving clockwise, stamped out a slow beat.

"What are they doing?" Oaf asked the fox. "And why?"

"It rewinds them when they have been sad or troubled."

"Well," said the crow crossly, "tell them to stop. They're giving me a headache."

"I can't," said the fox. "They've no future, you know, once we're imprisoned. The master will never forgive them for making a fool of him."

Before any of them could respond, a voice, hoarse as the

scrape of wheels on gravel, vibrant as thunder, shook the walls. It was the master singing.

> *"Give me a bone*
> *and I'll bite to the marrow;*
> *Give me an eagle,*
> *I'll size him to sparrow;*
>
> *Show me a mountain,*
> *I'll pummel it flat;*
> *I'm the best of the worst*
> *and that, chums, is that!"*

As if the first round weren't enough to satisfy him, he bellowed it again and then again until even Oaf felt his legs weaken and his hands tremble.

He shut his eyes and tried to remember his aunt but no image rose in his mind, only a gathering gray cloud that pressed at his temples.

No one slept. Even after the dreadsome singing ceased, the wakefulness in the caravan seemed to thicken the air they breathed. The dog scratched at imaginary fleas. The cat licked her paws as if she were attempting to remove the fur. The crow pecked a little tattoo on the floor. The rat's whiskers quivered as though teased by a brisk draft and the fox simply rested his head on his forelegs and sank into a kind of waking nightmare.

Only Oaf clung to the last twig of hope. He removed his cap and held it to his cheek. Then he carefully settled it once more onto his head and concentrated. At first only the terrible thought of the tower blocked his mind in its high blackness, the narrow slits of windows seeming to spew out evil as real as oil. Despair tugged at him and each word the fox had spoken of the horrors inside its round height resounded in his ears. The dwarfs would be put to death. Then his turn would come. The cages would fill and now Oaf could hear the cries and screams of the victims. And, worst of all, he imagined the master chortling his delight in their agony.

He almost snatched the cap from his head, unable to bear another instant of these visions, when suddenly the voice of his aunt came again and this time with only that one word: "Fifty-fifty." He opened his eyes to the interior of the caravan. He understood the message. Even with only half a chance they had to try.

He went to the fox and asked him to listen. As Oaf's words multiplied, the fox came alive. He sat up straight and his eyes began to glisten. Next Oaf summoned the dog, who forgot the fleas. The cat stood up, her tail active as a tiger's. The crow cawed strongly, twice, and the rat jigged as he listened.

Oaf took the matches he had found in a cupboard and called out, "Everybody ready?" With one stroke he lit the rag the crow had used for the Terror's costume. It flared into small flames and soon a curtain of smoke obscured the doorway.

The dog, obedient to Oaf's suggestion, began to growl, a sound so menacing that the dwarfs all held hands. He interspersed the growls with a throaty bark while the cat yowled her most piercing, the crow squawked, and the rat sent out small shrieks.

The noise was so ear-splitting Oaf had to shout to reach the ears of the master.

"Help! Help! Fire! The caravan's on fire!"

A tempest of curses flowed from the driver's seat and around to the door of the caravan. It burst open and the master loomed just outside, his whip raised.

But before he could enter, the dog lunged and seized the master's right leg in his jaws. The man brought the whip down on his back but the dog held on.

At that instant the crow arrowed at the master's head, clamping down with his claws. He drove his sharp beak into the master's skull, plucking out clumps of hair. The master shrieked and tried to shake him off but the crow held on.

Now the cat was riding the man's back, digging into his jacket and swiping at his neck, leaving long bloodied lines on the coarse skin. The master swatted at him with his fists but the cat held on.

The rat leaped into the air and up the master's left sleeve. He nipped and wriggled. The master screamed and banged his arm against his side but the rat held on.

Now the fox charged with all his strength directly at the man's stomach. The master staggered but did not fall. The fox charged again, this time receiving the slash of the whip on his flanks, but he charged a third time.

As though attached to the fox now Oaf joined the fray.

He lowered his head and threw himself at the giant of a man, colliding with the fox. The master fell.

Oaf tumbled off. The fox slid to one side. The master swiped at the crow, dislodging him, and managed to grasp the cat around the neck. He squeezed until the cat let go. With his left boot he aimed a kick at the dog, catching him in the ribs. The dog, choking, released his hold.

He flailed his whip in a circle like a scythe. The cutting whirl of it landed first on the fox's rump, then stung the cat's rear legs, caught the crow on his left wing, and flicked the dog across the eyes. The rat dropped out of his sleeve, squealing.

But Oaf, pushing with all his might to keep the master from getting up, got the worst of it. Once, twice, three times the whip descended across his chest. All was lost. Tears of pain streaking his face, he rolled against a wall.

The man began to rise but he had not lifted himself two feet when suddenly a clutter of arms and legs and heads descended upon him, pummeling him everywhere. He lay helpless, pinned by the weight of the five dwarfs, the queen straddling his forehead. And just then came the rat, who had directed the dwarfs, dragging the end of a long cord.

Oaf grabbed it and in three minutes the man was tied by the wrists and ankles. Oaf and the dwarfs dragged him out to the side of the caravan and propped him into a sitting position.

"Now," said Oaf, standing as erect as a general before the defeated master, "we will strike a bargain with you that you

But Oaf, pushing with all his might to keep the master from getting up, got the worst of it.

must keep or experience once more our power."

"I'd rather beat him than bargain," said the rat.

"Hush," said the crow. "Oaf is no fool."

Oaf did not pause to relish the rat's statement. "We will spare your life," he said, "in exchange for absolute freedom from you, dwarfs and all."

"Is that wise?" said the cat. "He might promise a hundred promises and keep none."

"I think not," said the dwarf queen as she pinched the master's chin with a twist that made him grunt. "With no one to bully he'll soon shrink to a less threatening size."

"Look," said the dog. "He's already shrinking."

"That's just because he's frightened," explained the rat. "Happens to everyone."

"Then if he stays frightened he'll get smaller," said the cat, purring her pride in her logic.

"Let's stop this palaver," said the fox, "and put it to a vote whether we leave this carcass to feast the buzzards or trust him to keep his promise."

"But he hasn't promised anything!" protested the rat.

"You will promise or else," stated Oaf, staring into the master's eyes.

The master, although he could understand nothing of this discussion, had had his fill and more of the hostility that surrounded him. He huddled lower. "I promise! I promise!" he spluttered. "Anything at all!"

"Take your time," said the fox to the others, ignoring the pleas of the master.

They took the hint and each one delayed voicing his vote,

the dog pacing thoughtfully up and down in front of the prostrate man, the cat studying her paws, the crow jerking his head back and forth as if contemplating an attack, the rat simply grinning as if he were enjoying something unthinkable, while the fox stared right into the master's eyes. The dwarfs hummed angrily in unison like oversize wasps.

"Those who vote to let him go on condition that his shadow never crosses ours again step forward and tell us why," said the fox.

The dog was first. "Ever since I was booted out I've known what it was to have no home but the thousand roads all leading nowhere except, when I was lucky, to the next meal. Now the master will have to learn the ways of hunger and homelessness. I believe that is punishment enough." He paused, slightly embarrassed by the length of his speech. "I vote to let him go."

The cat raised one paw for attention. "I'm for comfort. For the warm corners of the world where I can sit and lick my coat and dream of clotted cream. The master will look a long, long time before he finds such peace and plenty. For me that is punishment enough."

The crow was brief. "He can't fly like me, so if he ever plays a dastardly turn on anyone at all we can catch him. He will fear us forever. That, for me, is punishment enough."

The rat spoke quickly. "I'm worldly enough to wish him ill. He deserves the worst. But I think he has it now—no caravan, no troupe, nothing but what he must beg for and that, to me, is punishment enough."

The animals and Oaf looked to the fox but he had become a statue of himself, so still did he stand.

"All voting against," said the rat, "step sideways."

With one surge the dwarfs stepped sideways.

"I've something to say," said the queen, her head high, her back rigid. "And I'll say it once and not again."

The waiting silence was complete. Nothing stirred except the trembling of the master's hands.

"He must be put in his own cage and left to rot."

The dwarfs cheered and for an instant the fox's eyes gleamed red.

"Oh, please," groaned the master, who knew now that his life was in question, sweat shining on his pallid face. "Spare me. I promise to go where you will never see or hear of me again."

"The fox has not spoken," said Oaf.

The fox began softly. "There have been moments of pain and despair when I wished the master's death. He has scarred my memory with cruelties I cannot forget. But if I chose to scar him I would be no better than he, and my pride will not allow that to happen. I could not honor myself, and I need that honor more than an act of vengeance."

The animals looked at Oaf. The vote was five against five. He would have to decide it.

"How strange"—Oaf was talking to himself—"fifty-fifty. And now it's up to me."

He stood silent, remembering the master's cruelty, how he had been willing to see the dwarfs as slaves, how he had whipped the fox without mercy, his plans for their torture in the tower.

Oaf opened his mouth to cast his vote with the dwarfs when something seemed to touch him, first on one cheek and then on the other, something as light as a leaf but as warm as love and he never knew whether the voice that spoke "I vote to let him go" was his own or a gentler voice of long ago.

He looked down and saw that the fox was looking up at him. "You are wiser than a hundred foxes," he said.

Oaf laughed so that he wouldn't cry. "Let's untie him," he said. The dwarfs, although disappointed to be cheated of their revenge, helped undo the knots.

The master struggled upright and leaned weakly against the side of the caravan. Then, limping as fast as he could, he began to walk into the distance, and they watched his tallness diminish, yard by yard, until he was nothing but a tiny mark on the horizon and then nothing at all.

"Come on," said the crow. "Inside, everyone."

They all piled into the caravan except Oaf, who settled himself in the driver's seat behind the mule.

"I'll give a reception when I'm settled," said the queen proudly.

In an instant they were jerking unsteadily forward and Oaf could hear, over the clip-clop of the mule's hoofs, his comrades cheering him onward in a medley of tones.

As he finally fell into the rhythm of the road he thought again of his beloved aunt and remembered her words. "The last gift is a treasure. There is no known road and the way is steep, but one day you may be led to it."

"The last gift is a treasure. There is no known road and the way is steep, but one day you may be led to it."

Just then the crow joined him and perched on his shoulder, chuckling. "You know that treasure you told us about? Well, I used to dream of trees with diamond branches and emeralds growing on them like apples. Just dreams, mind you. And lesser ones like five chests bursting with gold pieces."

Oaf laughed.

"But," continued the crow, "I know better now. We've got it already, all of us." He flew to the mule's rump and hopped a small jig. And as Oaf listened to the others who were singing several songs at once, he smiled and waved toward the first stars.

ABOUT THE AUTHOR
AND THE ILLUSTRATOR

JULIA CUNNINGHAM's beautifully written novels and animal fantasies have earned her a loyal readership as well as distinguished honors, including a Christopher Award for *Come to the Edge* in 1977. Her most recent book, *Wolf Roland,* was hailed by *Booklist* as "a fable so well written it is a prize in itself."

Julia Cunningham was born in Spokane, Washington, grew up in New York City and Charlottesville, Virginia, and began her career as a writer while living in France. In addition to writing, she enjoys traveling and gets great pleasure from talking with children at schools and libraries around the country. She now lives in Santa Barbara, California.

PETER SIS is an illustrator and filmmaker. He was born in Czechoslovakia and studied at the Academy of Applied Arts in Prague and at the Royal College of Art in London. Since coming to this country he has illustrated several books for children, including *Bean Boy* by George Shannon, and his work has appeared regularly in *The New York Times Book Review* as well as *Atlantic Monthly, Esquire,* and *Discover.* His paintings have been exhibited in one-man shows in Prague, Zurich, and London and in group shows in Berlin and Los Angeles. He lives in New York City.